The Know How Book of Experiments

Heather Amery

Illustrated by Colin King

Contents

Educational Consultants:

Frank Blackwell
Patrick Eve
Evelyn Bourne

First published in 1977
Usborne Publishing Ltd
Usborne House, 83-85 Saffron Hill,
London EC1N 8RT, England

© Usborne Publishing Ltd 1989, 1977

Printed in Italy

About This Book

This book is for everyone who likes finding out about things, why they work and why they happen. It is full of experiments to discover the secrets of ordinary things, such as clouds and rain, plants and noises, as well as extraordinary things, such as rainbows and lightning.

There is always a reason why things happen in the way they do. But the reasons are not always simple and easy to understand. Even scientists cannot explain everything and there are still some mysteries to be solved.

All the experiments are absolutely safe to do, although some may surprise you and some are a bit messy. Some are very quick but others take quite a long time to work, so you will have to be very patient. When you have done the experiments, you may be able to think of some of your own to try.

For the experiments you will need paper, jars, bottles, balloons, big baking trays, plastic bags, string and plasticine. You can probably find them, as well as glue, sticky tape and scissors, at home.

This is Professor Bumble and his team

2

Amazing Ping Pong Ball

Here is some real science magic. Try these two experiments on your friends and surprise them. You need a drinking straw with a bend in it and a very small funnel. Or you can make your own. And you need lots of puff.

You will need
a ping pong ball
a piece of paper about 20 cm long and 10 cm wide
a circle of thin cardboard about 10 cm across
a bit of drinking straw, about 4 cm long
glue, sticky tape and scissors

TAKE A DEEP BREATH AND BLOW FOR AS LONG AS YOU CAN.

Hold the ping pong ball above the end of the straw. Take a deep breath and blow hard. Let go of the ball and it will stay there.

Put the ping pong ball into the funnel. Blow hard, pointing the funnel up. Keep blowing and point it down. The ball will stay in it.

1 Making a Tube

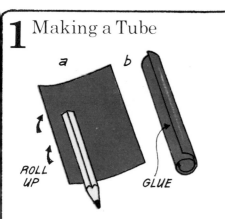

ROLL UP

GLUE

Put a pencil down on the edge of the piece of paper (a). Roll up the paper round it. Stick the edge with glue to make a long tube (b). Shake out the pencil.

Making a Funnel

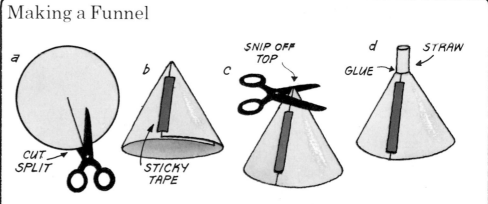

SNIP OFF TOP

GLUE   STRAW

CUT SPLIT

STICKY TAPE

Cut a slit from the edge of the cardboard circle to the middle (a). Curl the circle up to make a cone (b). Stick the edges, inside and outside, with tape.

Snip the top off the cone (c), to make a small hole in it. Push the bit of straw through the hole so it just goes down inside (d). Glue it to the cone. Leave to dry.

2

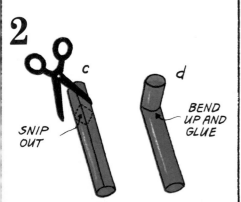

c   d

BEND UP AND GLUE

SNIP OUT

Make a small snip in the tube, near one end (c). Then make another snip to cut out a V-shaped bit. Bend up the end, like this, and spread glue round the join (d). Leave to dry.

Why It Works

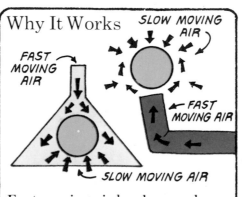

SLOW MOVING AIR

FAST MOVING AIR

FAST MOVING AIR

SLOW MOVING AIR

Fast moving air has less push or pressure than slow moving air. When you blow, air under the ball moves more slowly than air above it. This means there is more pressure upwards and the ball stays in the funnel.

Did You Know?

SLOW MOVING AIR

FAST MOVING AIR

SLOW MOVING AIR

Aircraft wings are curved on the top. When a plane is flying, air on top moves faster than air underneath and has less pressure. The slower air underneath has more push and helps to lift the plane and hold it up.

Bubble Boat

Make this boat and it will bubble its way round the bath under its own power. If you bend the tube at the back to one side, you can make the boat go round a corner.

You will need
a plastic bottle with a top
baking soda (this is used in cooking)
vinegar
thin paper or a paper tissue
plastic drinking straw or empty ink tube from an old ball-point pen
plasticine and scissors

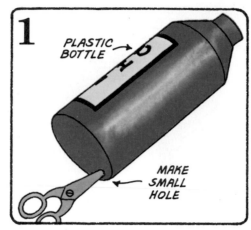

With scissors, make a small hole in the bottom of the plastic bottle, close to the edge.

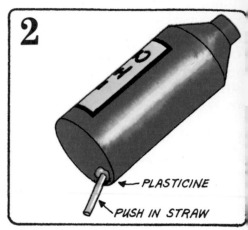

Push the plastic straw through the hole until only about 1 cm sticks out. Press the straw down a little. Press plasticine round it to keep it in place and fill up the hole.

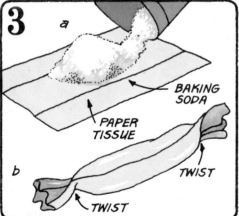

Shake some baking soda on to a paper tissue or piece of paper (a). Wrap the paper round the soda and twist the ends, like this (b).

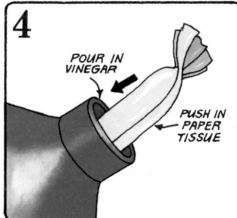

Pour some vinegar into the bottle. Push in the paper with the soda. Put the top on as quickly as you can. Put the bottle gently into a bath of water and let go.

PUT THE BOAT IN THE BATH AND IT WILL GO ALONG BY ITSELF.

Why It Works

When the paper gets wet in the vinegar, it untwists. The soda and vinegar mix together and make a lot of gas and foam. The gas goes out through the plastic straw and pushes the boat along.

Gas Cannon

Try making this bottle cannon and wait for the cork to blow out with a pop. You need baking soda which you may find in the kitchen cupboard, or you can buy it at a grocery shop.

You will need
a small glass bottle with a
   tightly fitting cork
baking soda
vinegar
piece of paper
water

1

Put some baking soda into the bottle. A good way to do this is to use a creased piece of paper and slide it in, like this.

2

Dip the cork in water to make it very wet. Pour some vinegar into the bottle and push in the cork as quickly as you can. Stand back and wait for the cork to pop out.

HOLD ON AND WAIT FOR THE CORK TO BLOW OUT.

Why It Works

Baking soda is a chemical, called sodium bicarbonate. When it mixes with vinegar, it makes a gas called carbon dioxide. This gas pushes the cork out of the bottle.

Did You Know?

Most explosives work because a special mixture of chemicals makes a huge amount of gas very quickly. The blast of gas blows things up with a bang.

Some rockets work in the same way. The fuel in them makes a great blast of gas. This spurts out the end of the rocket and pushes it up and along in space.

Magic Balloon Bottle

Set up this bottle experiment and amaze your friends. You can make it go on working as long as you like by just putting the bottle into hot water and then into cold water and then back again into the hot.

You will need
a bottle—any sort will do
a balloon
scissors
a bowl of hot water from the hot tap
· a bowl of very cold water

1

Fill the bottle with hot water from the hot tap. Leave it for a few minutes to warm the bottle. Pour out the water.

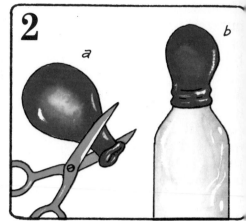

2

Cut the neck off the balloon (a). Stretch the balloon over the top of the bottle and pull it down (b). Stand the bottle in the bowl of cold water. Now watch.

Why It Works

When you warm the bottle with hot water, the air in the bottle is warmed. When air is warmed it gets bigger. This is called expansion. When you cool the bottle with cold water, the air in it is cooled and gets smaller. This is called contraction. As the air gets smaller, the air outside pushes the balloon into the bottle. If you warm up the bottle again, the air inside expands and pushes the balloon out again.

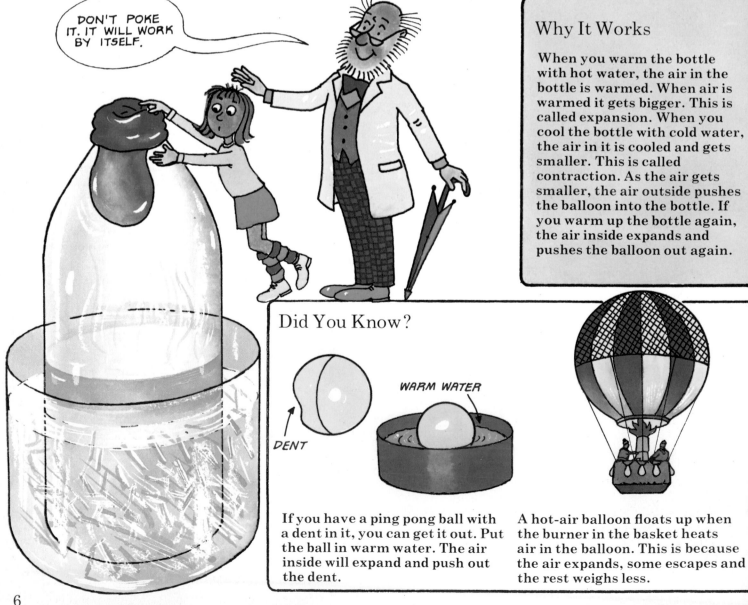

DON'T POKE IT. IT WILL WORK BY ITSELF.

Did You Know?

DENT

WARM WATER

If you have a ping pong ball with a dent in it, you can get it out. Put the ball in warm water. The air inside will expand and push out the dent.

A hot-air balloon floats up when the burner in the basket heats air in the balloon. This is because the air expands, some escapes and the rest weighs less.

Bottle Fountain

Here is another surprise to puzzle your friends. You will have to tell them why it works because they will never guess.

You will need
a small bottle with a screw-on
   top
a plastic drinking straw
plasticine
a pin or needle
poster paint or ink
a bowl of very hot water

1

COLD WATER   MAKE HOLE

Take the top off the bottle. Make a hole in the top with scissors, pressing downwards, like this. Half fill the bottle with cold water.

2

INK OR POSTER PAINT   SCREW ON TOP

Pour a few drops of poster paint or ink into the water in the bottle. Screw the top on very tightly.

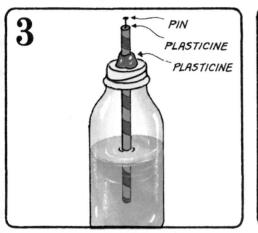

3

PIN
PLASTICINE
PLASTICINE

Push the straw through the hole. Press plasticine round it to seal up the hole. Put a plug of plasticine in the end of the straw. Poke a hole in it with a pin or needle.

4

HOT WATER

Put the bottle in a bowl and fill it up with very hot water from the hot tap. Wait a while for the fountain to work.

Why It Works

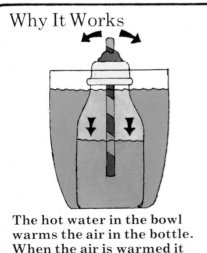

The hot water in the bowl warms the air in the bottle. When the air is warmed it expands and pushes the water up the straw and out in a spray.

THE BOTTLE MAKES A GOOD FOUNTAIN.

7

Grow Your Own Crystals

You can grow crystals by stirring salt, sugar or washing soda into very hot water. Leave them to grow in a warm place and every day you will see a few more until there are lots clinging together in a lump.

You will need
a clean glass jar
a long piece of thread
a paper clip
washing soda (you may find it in your kitchen or you can buy it at a grocery shop)
very hot water from the tap
a pencil

Put a spoon into the jar to stop the hot water cracking it. Run the hot tap a little and then fill up the jar with water.

Put several teaspoons of washing soda into the water and stir until it has all disappeared. Put in more soda and stir again.

Stand the jar in a bowl of very hot water to keep the water in the jar hot. Spoon in more soda and stir again. Stir in soda until no more will disappear in the water.

Tie a paper clip on to one end of a piece of thread. Tie the other end round a pencil. Drop the clip into the jar. Wind the thread round the pencil until the clip hangs like this.

Try mixing a few drops of poster paint or ink in the water to make coloured crystals.

LEAVE THE JAR FOR A FEW DAYS AND THE CRYSTALS WILL GROW BIGGER AND BIGGER.

Did You Know?

Lots of things, such as sugar, salt, sand and precious stones are crystals. Each crystal has its own shape. You can see them with a magnifying glass.

Crystal Columns

Here is a way to make pillars of soda grow up and down until they meet in the middle. It takes several days to work so you will have to be patient.

You will need
glass jars
washing soda and a spoon
lengths of wool, each about 35 cm long, twisted together to make a thick string
hot water from the hot tap
a large, old plate

1
a
b WASHING SODA

Fill two jars with very hot water. Stir in lots of washing soda. Go on stirring it in until no more will disappear in the water.

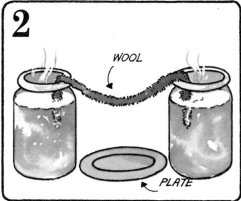

2
WOOL
PLATE

Put the two jars somewhere warm where they will not be moved. Put the plate in between them. Drop the ends of the wool into the jars so the wool hangs over the plate.

Why It Works

Water and soda from the jars goes along the wool and drips off the middle. As it drips, the water turns into tiny drops, so small you cannot see them, in the air. The soda is left in a hard drip.

Did You Know?

The pillars in caves, called stalagmites and stalactites, are made in the same way as the soda column. Water, with lime from limestone rocks, drips from the ceiling. As the water goes into the air, it leaves the lime behind which builds up over hundreds of years, very, very slowly.

The stalagmites are the ones growing up from the floor. The stalactites grow down from the ceiling.

AFTER A FEW DAYS, THE COLUMNS WILL MEET IN THE MIDDLE.

Air is Everywhere

You cannot see air but it fills nearly every space and crack in the world. When anything looks empty, it is really full of air. Air is a gas which you cannot feel except when the wind blows or when you breathe in and out. There is a thick layer of air all round the earth. This layer has a lot of weight and pushes on everything around us.

You will need
2 glasses and a bowl of water
a thin piece of wood, about 45 cm long and about 4 cm wide
2 sheets of a large newspaper
a hammer or mallet

PUSH GLASS DOWN

An empty glass looks as if it has nothing in it. To show it is full of air, hold it down in a bowl of water, like this. The air keeps nearly all the water out.

Now tilt the glass a little. The air bubbles up through the water and the water fills the glass. Try catching the air in a filled glass under the water, like this.

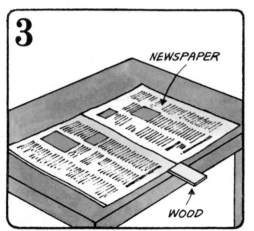

NEWSPAPER

WOOD

Put the thin piece of wood on the table, with a bit sticking over the edge. Spread out two sheets of newspaper over it. Smooth them down so they are very flat.

NOW HIT THE WOOD AS HARD AS YOU CAN.

Did You Know?

The pressure in your body equals the air pressure pushing all over you. Men on the moon or in space, where there is no air, have to wear suits with pressure in them.

Why It Works

AIR PRESSING ON PAPER

When you hit the wood, the air pressing down on the newspaper is too heavy to be lifted up, so the wood breaks. The push of air round us is called atmospheric pressure.

Hit the thin piece of wood very hard with a hammer or mallet. Do it quickly and the wood snaps.
If you just press down on the bit of wood, the newspaper will lift up as the air gets in under the paper. So give the wood a good bang.

Is Air Heavy?

Here is a good way to find out if air weighs anything. It is difficult to take all the air out of a tin or bottle without special equipment but you can do it with balloons.

You will need
a thin stick, about 60 cm long
2 balloons, which are the same size and shape
3 pieces of string, each about 30 cm long
a pin

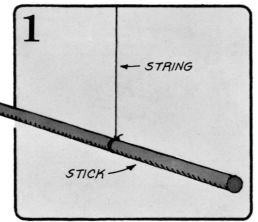

1 Tie the end of one string tightly to the middle of the stick. Hang the stick up by the other end. Slide the string along the stick until it hangs exactly level.

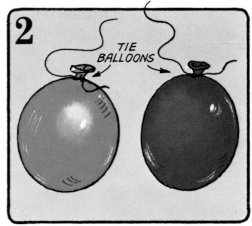

2 Blow up one balloon and tie the neck with a second string. Blow up the second balloon until it is about the same size as the first. Tie the neck with a third string.

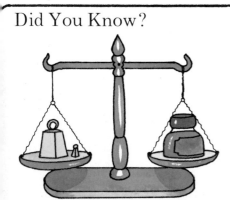

3 Tie a balloon on to each end of the stick. Slide the strings along the stick until the stick hangs exactly level again. Now prick one balloon with a pin and watch.

Did You Know?

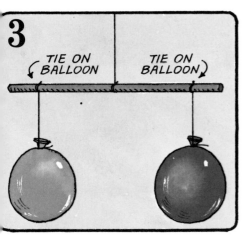

If you weighed a bottle which holds one litre of air and then took all the air out and weighed it again, the bottle with air would weigh one gram more than the bottle without.

Why It Works

NOW BURST THE OTHER BALLOON AND SEE WHAT HAPPENS.

When you burst one balloon, all the air comes out. The other balloon with air in weighs more than the empty one, so the stick goes down.

Now burst the other balloon and the stick will become level again.

Can You Believe Your Eyes?

If you can see something, then you know it is real—unless it is magic, of course. Here are a few ways to test whether your eyes are telling you the truth or if they sometimes deceive you. Try these tricks yourself and then ask other people to do them. You will need a ruler to check the answers. You may be in for a few surprises. Keep a score of the ones you get right.

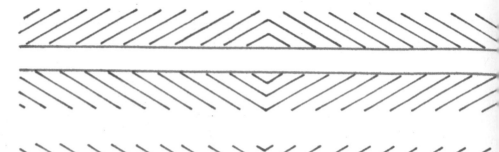

Are all the green lines straight or do they bend a bit? Do the top ones get wider at each end? Do the underneath ones get wider in the middle? To find out, put the edge of a ruler along each green line.

USE A RULER TO MEASURE ALL THE LINES.

Look at these two shapes. Is the top red line longer than the lower red line? Measure them with a ruler to find the answer.

Are these two red lines the same length? Use a ruler to find out.

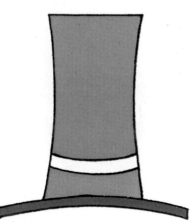

This is a funny hat but is it as high as the brim is wide?

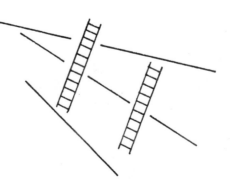

Which of these two ladders is the longer one; or are they both the same length?

Why It Works

When we look at things, our brains are sometimes fooled by them. These things are called optical illusions which means we see things which are not really true.

When you look at the green lines at the top of this page, your eyes are misled by the red lines, so the green lines look bent. It is the same with all the other tricks. When you measure them with a ruler, you find all the lines are the same length. How many did you get right?

ere are some more tricks to
lay with your eyes. Try them
ourself first. Then tell other
eople how to do them but don't
ll what they will see so they
et a surprise. You can always
retend it is a bit of magic that
nly you can do.

or the Hole in Your Hand
ick you need a paper or
rdboard tube. You can make
ne out of a sheet of paper.

loating Finger

STARE HARD JUST BEYOND YOUR FINGERS.

old one finger of each hand up in
ront of your eyes, like this. Stare
ard between them.

ole in Your Hand

LOOK DOWN THE TUBE AND KEEP THE OTHER EYE OPEN.

old a tube up to your right eye.
old your left hand up beside the
be, like this. Stare very hard
wn the tube.

How Many Fingers?

Hold one finger of each hand up in
front of your eyes, about 20 cm
away from your face. Stare at
something beyond your fingers, not
at them.

You Will See

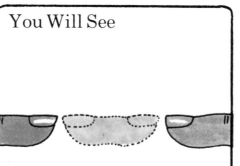

If you stare hard at the gap
between your fingers, you will
see a short finger appear
between them. The odd thing
about it is that it has a nail
on each end.

Making a Tube

ROLL UP

30 cm

21 cm

Make a tube by rolling up a sheet
of stiff paper, about 30 cm long and
20 cm wide. Stick the edge with
sticky tape or glue.

You Will See

If you stare hard, you will see
three or four ghostly fingers in
front of your eyes. Look at
your two fingers and the other
two will disappear.

Why It Works

You see four fingers in the
How Many Fingers? trick
because you are looking
beyond your fingers. So you
see two fingers with each eye,
making four in all. With the
Floating Finger trick, the two
extra fingers overlap to make
an extra finger in the middle.
You see a hole in your hand
because one eye is looking
down the tube and the other is
looking at your hand. These
two views mix together so you
see a hand with a hole in it.
They all work because you
have two eyes.

You Will See

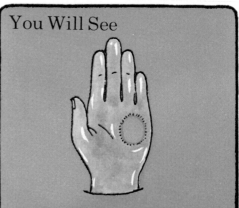

Stare hard down the tube with
your right eye, keeping your
left eye open. You can see your
hand and then you will see a
hole you can look through.

Seeing the Invisible

You cannot see noises—even nice ones like music or nasty ones like the screeching of car brakes—but you hear them all the time. There is always noise of some sort and, if you listen hard, you can always hear something. Here are two ways to find out about noise.

You will need
a thin plastic bag
a big tin or bowl
a rubber band
bits of paper and some sugar
a big spoon and a baking tray
a wine glass
a piece of silver foil and thread

BANG THE TRAY AS HARD AS YOU CAN. WATCH THE SUGAR JUMP!

1 Jumping Paper

THIN PLASTIC
RUBBER BAND
BIG TIN

Cut along one side and the bottom of a plastic bag. Spread it tightly over the top of a big tin or bowl. Stretch a rubber band round the tin or bowl to make a drum.

2

BITS OF PAPER

Tear up a piece of paper into very small bits. Put them on top of the drum. Tap the drum with a spoon. and the bits of paper will jump.

3 Jumping Sugar

BAKING TRAY
SUGAR

Sprinkle some sugar on top of the drum. Hold the baking tray close to the drum. Hit the tray hard with a big spoon. Watch carefully and you will see the sugar jump.

1 Jumping Ball

THREAD
TAPE
SILVER FOIL

Put a wine glass down on a table but don't use one of the best ones. Scrunch up a bit of foil into a ball. Stick a piece of thread, about 30 cm long, to it with tape.

2

WINE GLASS

Hold up the thread so the foil ball just hangs against the edge of the glass, like this. Tap the glass gently with a pencil and the ball will jump away.

Why It Works

When you hit the drum, tray or glass, they all waggle when they make a noise. This waggle is called vibration and makes the paper, sugar and foil ball jump about. When anything vibrates it makes the air round it vibrate. The air then carries the vibration from the thing to your ears so you hear a noise.
You can sometimes feel sound with your fingers. If you put your hand lightly on a radio or record player which is on very loud, you can feel it vibrating.

High and Low Notes

When you play a tune on a musical instrument, you have to make different notes. If the instrument has strings, you press them with your fingers. If it is an instrument you blow, you put your fingers over the holes to play a tune. Here are two ways to find out about music—even if you cannot play anything.

You will need
a wooden ruler
a rubber band
2 pencils

VERY BIG INSTRUMENTS MAKE LOW NOTES. LITTLE ONES MAKE HIGH NOTES.

1 Noisy Ruler

PULL DOWN AND LET GO

Put a ruler on a table, with most of it over the edge, like this. Hold the part on the table down with a book. Pull the other end down and let it go. It makes a low twang.

2

PULL DOWN AND LET GO

Push the ruler in under the book a bit and pull it down again. It makes a higher twang. Push it in a bit more and the noise gets higher. You can see the ruler waggling.

1 Ruler Guitar

RUBBER BAND

PENCIL

PENCIL

Stretch a long rubber band over a ruler, like this. Push a pencil under the band at one end and a second pencil under the band at the other end.

Why It Works

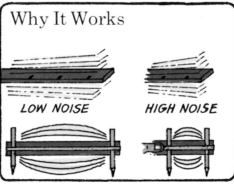

LOW NOISE   HIGH NOISE

When a ruler or band is long, it vibrates slowly and makes a low noise. When it is short, it vibrates quickly and makes high noises. High and low sounds depend on how fast things vibrate.

2

SLIDE PENCIL ALONG

Pluck the band with one finger. Push one pencil along the ruler a bit and pluck the band again. It will make a higher note. You can play a tune—very slowly.

Did You Know?

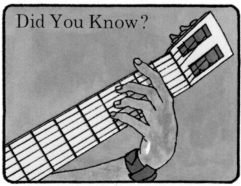

Players of string instruments press the strings to shorten them and make higher notes. They tighten or loosen the strings before they play. Tight strings vibrate more quickly and make higher notes.

Water Tricks

All light—light from the sun, from electric light and from fires—usually travels in straight lines. If it could go round corners, there would be no shadows when the sun shines or shadows in a room. But light does strange things when it goes through the air and then through water. Here are some ways to find out what it does.

You will need
a glass of water and a straw or a pencil
a bowl of water and a coin

THE STRAW LOOKS QUITE STRAIGHT FROM HERE.

Put a straw or a pencil into a glass of water. Hold the glass up level with your eyes and the straw or pencil will look broken.

1 Magic Coin

DROP IN COIN

Drop a small coin into a china or plastic bowl. Tilt the bowl until you cannot quite see the coin over the edge.

2

WATER

Hold the bowl in exactly the same position so you still cannot quite see the coin. Pour water slowly into the bowl and the coin will gradually reappear.

Moving Coin

MOVE UP AND DOWN

Now hold the bowl up so you can see the coin. Move the bowl slowly up and down, staring at the coin. As you watch, it seems to move up and down in the bowl.

Why It Works

Light going through air and then through water at an angle, bends as it goes into water and out again. This makes the straw look broken and the coin reappear in the bowl.

Did You Know?

A boy standing on a river bank, trying to catch a fish in the water, may miss the fish, unless he knows about light and water. The fish will look higher up in the water than it really is. This is because the light beams the boy sees have been bent by the water. The river will also look much shallower than it is.

Light Tricks

When you look down at a pool of still water you can see your own face in it. The water acts like a mirror. Before people knew how to make mirrors, they used bowls of water instead. If you could look up from underneath the water, the top of it would also act like a mirror. Try these ways of finding out about water.

You will need
a glass, water and a coin
a square glass or clear plastic
    container
water and a teaspoon of milk
a sheet of paper and a book
a torch

One or Two Coins?

Drop a small coin in a glass with water, about 2 cm deep, in it. Hold the glass up in front of your eyes. You will see a big coin on the bottom and a small one just above it in the water.

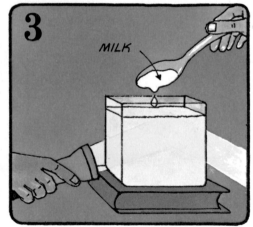

I CAN SEE ONLY ONE COIN. HOW MANY CAN YOU SEE?

1 Bouncing Beam

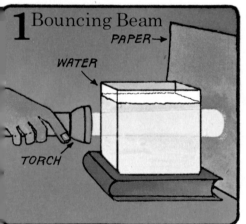

PAPER →
WATER
TORCH

Stand the square container, full of water, on a book. Prop up a sheet of paper at one end. Draw the curtains or switch off the light. Shine a torch like this.

2

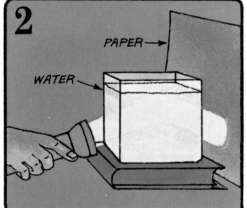

PAPER →
WATER

Shine the torch straight through and the beam comes out in a straight line. Shine the torch at an angle and the beam comes out at an angle on the paper.

3

MILK

To see the beam more clearly, stir a teaspoon of milk into the water. Then try shining the torch through the water from lots of different angles to see how the beam bends.

Why It Works

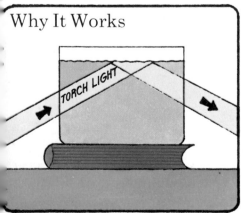

TORCH LIGHT

When light shines straight into water, it goes in a straight line. When a beam hits the top of the water at an angle, it is bounced back at an angle by the water.

Did You Know?

LAYER OF WARM AIR
LAYER OF HOT AIR
SUNLIGHT

On a very hot day, you sometimes see puddles on a road. When you get near, they vanish. These are called mirages and are seen in deserts. The man in this picture gets light from the sky. It is bent by a layer of hot air on the ground. He sees a reflection of sky and clouds on the ground, which looks like pools of blue water.

What Makes a Rainbow?

Look for rainbows in the sky when the sun is shining and it is raining at the same time. You can also see rainbows in the spray from garden hoses,

THE COLOURS OF A RAINBOW ARE ALWAYS IN THE SAME ORDER.

fountains and waterfalls. But to see rainbows, you have to stand with your back to the sun and facing the raindrops.

How to Make a Rainbow

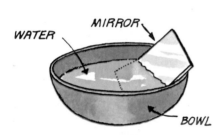

WATER
MIRROR
BOWL

You will have to do this on a sunny day. Fill a small bowl with water. Put a small mirror into the bowl so that the sun shines on to it.

Hold up a sheet of white paper so the sun shining on the mirror reflects on to the paper. Hold the paper as still as you can and you will see rainbow colours.

Why It Works

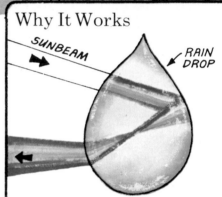

SUNBEAM
RAIN DROP

When sunlight goes through a water drop, it is split up into seven main colours, like this. That is why you see a rainbow when the sun shines on lots of drops of water.

Rainbow Colours in Glass

White light shining through glass with sharp angles in it is split up into colours. You can see some colours in precious stones, like diamonds, and in cut glass.

The best shape of glass for making colours is one like a tent, called a prism. The coloured light coming out of one prism is turned into white light by another.

Did You Know?

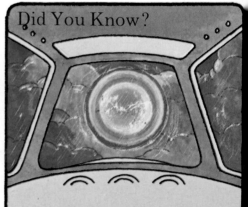

If you were in the cockpit of a plane flying towards a rain storm, with the sun behind you, you would see a moving rainbow. It would be a circle.

Disappearing Colours

You can make colours appear and disappear. Paint a circle with the seven colours of the rainbow and spin it very fast. Watch to see what happens.

THESE ARE THE MAIN COLOURS YOU SEE IN A RAINBOW.

1 Coloured Whirler

DRAW ROUND

Put a cup down on a thick piece of cardboard and draw round it. Cut round the line with scissors to make a neat circle.

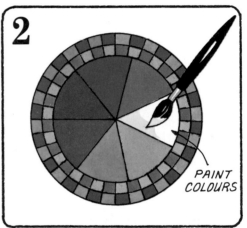

2

PAINT COLOURS

Draw six lines from the middle of the circle to the outside edge to make seven sections. Paint each section a colour of the rainbow, like the picture on the left.

The colours you see in a rainbow are called a spectrum. They are red, orange, yellow, green, blue, indigo and violet. There are lots of shades in between them.

You can paint the whirler just red, yellow, green and blue, if you like. The coloured squares on the outside of this one blur into the colours of the rainbow.

Why It Works

When the Whirler spins very fast, our eyes see the colours but they get mixed up in our brains. Our brains tell us the Whirler looks a greyish white.

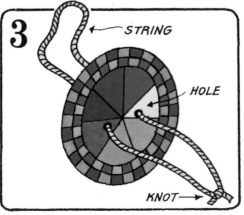

3

STRING

HOLE

KNOT

Make two holes in the circle, about 1 cm apart, like this. Push the ends of a piece of string, about a metre long, through the holes. Tie the ends in a knot.

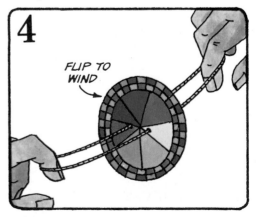

4

FLIP TO WIND

Hold the loops of string like this. Flip the circle round to twist up the string. Pull your hands apart and then let the string go slack. This will make the Whirler spin.

What Makes a Thunderstorm?

The different sorts of clouds you see in the sky mean that different sorts of weather are coming. When you see huge, tall clouds, like puffy castles, they may mean a thunderstorm is on its way, with flashes of lightning. A flash is a huge, hot electric spark. You can make a little one safely at home, but it may make your fingers prick and tingle a bit.

THOSE BIG CLOUDS MAY MEAN A THUNDERSTORM IS COMING.

1 Making a Spark

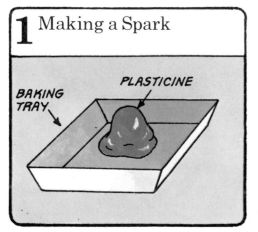

BAKING TRAY
PLASTICINE

Press a large lump of plasticine on to the middle of a very big baking tray or small tin tray. Press it hard so it sticks well.

2

PLASTIC BAG
RUB HARD

Put the tray down on a very large, thick plastic or polythene bag. A rubbish bag is good for this. Hold the plasticine lump and rub the tray round and round on the bag.

3

LIFT UP TRAY
TIN LID

Pick up the tray by the plasticine. Hold something metal, such as a tin lid, close to one corner. You will see a big spark jump from the tray to the tin especially in a dark room.

Why It Works

When you rub the tray on the bag, it makes electricity, called static electricity. When there is enough, there is a spark. Static electricity builds up in clouds before a thunderstorm.

Did You Know?

Most lightning flashes jump from one cloud to another. A few strike the earth and may do damage. Tall buildings have lightning conductors to carry the electricity safely down into the ground.

The thunder you hear after a flash is made by lightning. The spark heats the air round it and the air expands very quickly. This sets off a giant wave of air which makes the thunder you hear.

Why is a Sunset Red?

When the sun first rises in the morning, the sky often looks red, especially if there are a few clouds about. During the day, when the sun is overhead, it looks yellow and the sky looks blue. When the sun sets, it may turn a fiery red and the sky pink. Do they really change colour or just look as if they do? Here is a way to find out.

THE SUN IS BRIGHT RED NOW IT IS SO LOW ON THE SEA.

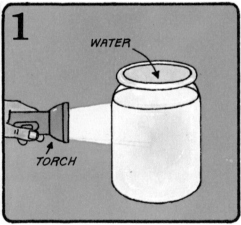

1 WATER TORCH

Fill a clean glass jar with cold water. Stir in one teaspoonful of milk. Hold a torch to the side of the jar, like this, in a dark room. The water looks blue.

2

Now move the torch round so it is shining through the jar at you, like this. The light from the torch looks yellow, like the sun during the day.

3 MILK AND WATER

Stir in two more teaspoonfuls of milk. Hold the torch to the side of the jar. The water still looks blue. Hold it so it shines at you and the water looks pink.

Why It Works

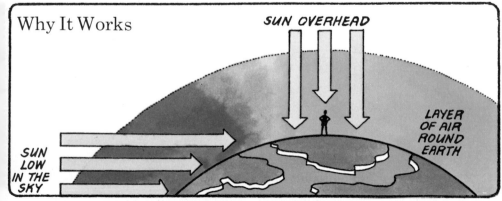

SUN OVERHEAD

SUN LOW IN THE SKY

LAYER OF AIR ROUND EARTH

The Earth is wrapped in a blanket of air which is full of bits of dust and water drops too small to see. The dust and water drops, like the milk in the glass of water, scatter the blue part of sunlight to make the sky look blue. When the sun is low in the sky, it looks red because its light has to go further through the air and only the red part of it comes through to your eyes.

Did You Know?

If you looked out of a window in a space ship, the sky would look black and you would see stars in the day. This is because there is no dusty air in space to break up white light into its colours.

Rubbing and Warming

Have you ever noticed that things get warm when you rub them? On cold days, people rub their hands together or rub their hands on their sleeves to warm them. Try it and your hands will soon warm up. There are lots of things which get warm and even very hot when they are rubbed. Here are a few for you to try. There are lots more you can probably think of yourself.

Try rubbing two dry sticks or bits of wood together as hard as you can. After about 20 rubs, feel the wood. It will be quite warm.

Rub two pieces of metal, such as flat tin lids, together. Rub a piece of wood with sandpaper. Feel the metal and wood after a minute or two and they will be quite hot.

RUB HARD AND THEN FEEL HOW WARM IT IS.

When you ride a bicycle and brake hard, the brake blocks rub on the wheel to slow you down. Try braking while riding quite slowly. Then feel the brake blocks.

Scuff your shoes hard across the floor. Then feel the bottoms of your shoes. Try rubbing your bare foot hard on a carpet. It will soon feel quite warm.

Why It Works

Most things have rough surfaces. You can see they are rough if you look at them closely or with a magnifying glass—your hands, wood and metal. When they move against each other, the roughness slows down the movement. This is called friction. The rougher two things are, the harder you have to work to move them. The work is turned into heat and the things become hot.

Did You Know?

Car tyres warm up because of the friction between them and the road. After a long journey, they may be too hot to touch. This warms the road too. Ice on roads melts if lots of cars go over it.

When a spacecraft returns to Earth, friction between it and the air makes it very hot. Its special shape and shield of special materials stop men inside from being burnt up.

Slipping and Gripping

The rough surfaces of lots of things are useful because they grip together and stop slipping. Your shoes grip a slippery floor. Bicycle brake blocks are made of special material to grip the wheel rim. Car tyres have ridges in them to help grip the road. But this grip is a nuisance when we want things to slide easily. Slippery oil is poured into machines so the moving bits slide over each other. Here are some ways to make things slip about very easily.

SHOES WITH SMOOTH SOLES SLIDE MORE EASILY THAN ROUGH SOLES.

The rough soles of your shoes stop you from slipping. You slide on ice because the pressure of your shoes melts the ice a little. You slide on a very thin sheet of water which then freezes again.

1

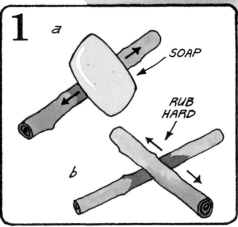

Find two dry sticks or bits of wood. Rub a piece of soap over one of them. Now rub the sticks together. They will slide over each other and stay cool.

2

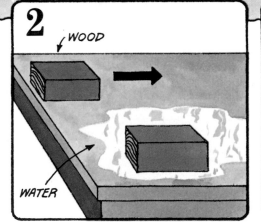

Put a small block of wood on a table. Give it a knock to make it slide (a). Pour a little soapy water on the table (b). Knock the block again to see what happens.

3

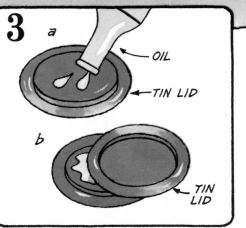

Pour a little oil on a flat tin lid. Any oil, such as cooking oil, will do. Rub the lid with another lid. You can feel the lids slide easily over each other on the oil.

Why It Works

Oil is poured on the moving bits of machines to keep them slightly apart. They slide over each other on a layer of slippery oil without touching, and do not get hot. This is called lubrication.

Did You Know?

Cars skid on greasy, wet or icy roads because grease, water or ice makes a layer between the tyres and the road. The tyres cannot grip so the car skids.

All machines with parts which slide over each other need oil or grease lubrication. Without it, they would rub and could get so hot they would melt.

Bottle Volcano

Here is a surprising trick to try with two bottles of water—one warm and the other cold.

You will need
2 clean glass bottles—ones with wide necks are best
cold water and warm water from the hot tap
a small square of cardboard
a few drops of ink or water paint.

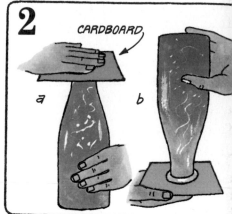

1

Fill one bottle with cold water and the other with warm water from the tap. Pour a few drops of ink or paint into the bottle with the warm water to colour it.

2

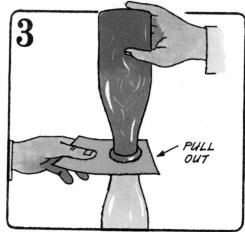

Put the square of cardboard over the top of the bottle with coloured water. Hold it on with one hand (a). Still holding it, turn the bottle over with the other hand (b).

3

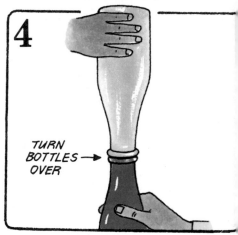

Put the bottle with coloured water on top of the other bottle, like this. They must be exactly on top of each other. Hold the top bottle and pull out the cardboard.

4

Hold both bottles like this. Turn them up the other way, without letting the tops slide apart and the water run out. Now watch.

Why It Works

Warm water is lighter than cold water so it floats on the top of cold water, like this. When you turn the bottles over, so the cold is on the top, it sinks down and pushes the warm, coloured water up.

Did You Know?

At the North and South Poles the very cold weather cools the top of the sea. The cold water sinks down, pushing up water from the bottom. Scientists think this may cause ocean currents.

Strong Ice

When water cools down and freezes into ice, something strange happens to it. For these experiments, you have to use the freezing compartment of a refrigerator. Use a plastic pot or a tin. Do not use glass or it will crack.

You will need
a small plastic pot with a lid
a small, clean tin with a lid
3 pencils
a bottle top
sticky tape
a refrigerator

Fill the plastic pot right to the top with cold water. Press on the lid. Put the pot in the freezing compartment of a refrigerator. Leave it for about eight hours.

Take out the pot. When the water has turned to ice, it lifts up the lid and pushes it off the pot. You may find the sides have been pushed out a bit too.

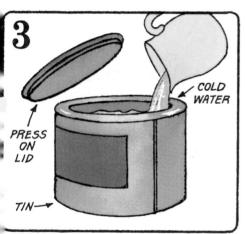

Fill a tin up to the top with cold water. Press on the lid as hard as you can, without spilling the water.

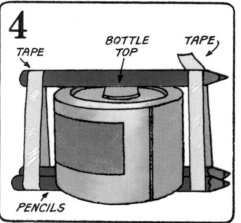

Put a bottle top on the lid. Put two pencils under the tin and one on the bottle top. Wind sticky tape round the pencils, like this. Freeze for about eight hours.

WHEN WATER FREEZES IT GETS BIGGER AND BREAKS VERY STRONG THINGS.

When the tin has been in the freezing compartment for about eight hours, have a look at it. You will find the lid has been pushed up by the ice and broken the pencil. The sides may have been pushed out as well.

Why It Works

When water cools and turns into ice it gets bigger and pushes outwards. It presses so hard that it breaks water pipes on the outside of houses in freezing weather.

Did You Know?

When rain runs into tiny cracks in rocks on mountains and then freezes into ice, the ice pushes so hard it splits the rock. That is why some mountain tops are covered with sharp, broken rocks.

Ups and Downs of Plants

If you plant a seed upside down, does it grow upside down? Or does it turn itself round and grow the right way? Try growing some beans or peas to find out what happens to the roots and stems.

You will need

6 beans or peas (the kind sold for growing, not for eating)

some earth—the sort sold in bags called potting compost is best)

a pot or bowl

a little plastic bottle

black paper, a rubber band and scissors

Fill the bowl or pot with earth or compost. Press it down with your fingers. Fill the bowl with water and wait until it has sunk into the earth.

Press the beans or peas into the earth. Put the bowl in a warm, ligh place and wait for the seeds to sprout. They will take about a week to split and grow.

When the seeds have sprouted, cut the top and bottom off a small plastic bottle. It should be big enough to slip a bean or pea in easily with room to spare.

Push one bean or pea into the bottle. Push damp earth in at each end. Pack it well round the seed. Drip on a little water at each end.

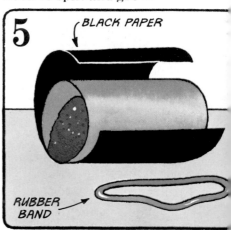

Wrap a bit of black paper round th bottle, leaving the ends open. Kee it in place with a rubber band. Put the bottle in a warm, light place. Look at it every day.

TURN THE BOTTLE FOR A DAY AND THE SHOOTS WILL GROW THE OTHER WAY.

When two shoots come out of the bottle, one grows up and has tiny green leaves. The other, the white root, grows down. Turn the bottle over for a day and a night. The shoots will grow the other way.

Why It Works

Whichever way you plant seeds, the stems will always grow up to the light. The roots always grow down into the earth for water and food.

Waterways of Plants

All plants need water to keep alive and to grow. They get the water through their roots and it goes up their stems. Plants also give out water through their leaves in such tiny drops you cannot see them. Try these experiments with plants.

You will need

a stick of fresh celery
a table knife
ink or water paint
a bush or branch of a tree growing out of doors
a plastic bag
a piece of string

1 Sucking up Water

Slice a bit off the end of the stick of celery. Put the stick in a jar with a little water. Pour in some ink. Stand the jar in a warm, light place for a day.

2

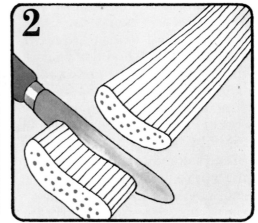

Wash the end of the celery stick in clean water. Slice the stem about every 3 cm. Look at each cut. You can see dots where the stem has taken up the coloured water.

1 Breathing Out Water

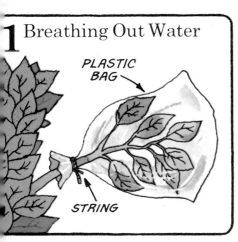

PLASTIC BAG

STRING

Put a plastic bag over a small branch of leaves on a bush or small tree in a sunny place. Tie it on with string, like this. Leave it for two or three days.

2

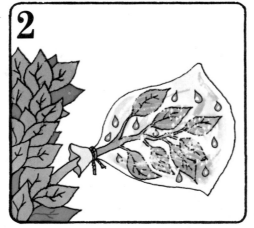

Look at the bag every day and you will see drops of water on the inside of the bag. If the days are very hot, quite a lot of water will collect in the bag.

Why It Works

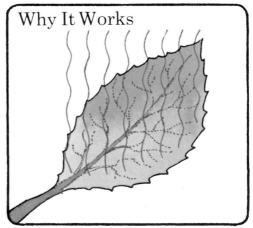

The leaves of plants have very tiny holes all over them. On hot days, tiny drops of water come out from these holes into the air. These collect on the inside of the bag.

Did You Know?

On a very hot day, a tree, such as a birch or elm, may take up as much as 50 large buckets of water. This comes out invisibly through its leaves into the air.

Try tying a plastic bag round a plant indoors. Water it and stand it on a windowsill in the sun.

YOU CAN CHANGE THE COLOUR OF A FLOWER WITH A LITTLE INK.

Try putting a white flower stem in coloured water. The petals will soon show the colour of the water.

Where Do Clouds Come From?

After a shower of rain, all the water on the roads, the grass, the houses and even your clothes, slowly dries up and disappears. The puddles get smaller and smaller until they vanish. The water disappears much more quickly when the weather is hot and sunny. When it is cold and damp, the wet things take much longer to dry. But where does the water go? And where do the rain clouds come from? How does all that water get into the sky to make rain? Here are ways to find out.

1 Water Into Air

Put a big plate on a sunny windowsill. Pour some cold water on to the plate. Leave it for three hours. Look at it often and you will see the water disappears.

2

Put two plates in a sunny place. Pour about half a cup of water on to each one. Shade one with a book, like this. Look at them after an hour or two to see what happens.

Why It Works

When water dries up, it turns into tiny drops, so small you cannot see them. This is called evaporation. The water drops go into the air. This damp air, called water vapour, rises. On warm days, it rises all the time, taking the vapour up to the sky. In the sky it is much cooler than down on the ground. The tiny drops of water join up to make bigger drops. These make the clouds you see in the sky.

Warm Air Goes Up

Cut a few strips of the thinnest paper you can find. Tissue paper or thin cellophane work well. Hold them over a radiator or room heater and they flutter upwards.

Did You Know?

On warm days, the water in clouds falls as rain. It runs into ponds, lakes, rivers and then to the sea. Water from all wet things, even clothes on a washing line, goes up into the air. In warm weather it goes up to make more clouds which may rain again.

Why Does It Rain?

Try these experiments and find out how water comes from warm damp air.

IT IS RAINING HERE BUT IT IS SNOWING HIGH ON THE MOUNTAINS.

1 Water from Air
COLD PLATE
HOT WATER

Fill a bowl with water from the hot tap. Hold a cold plate over the bowl for about a minute. Turn the plate over. It is covered with tiny drops of water.

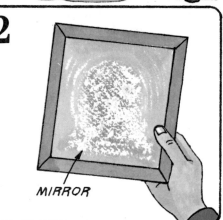

2
MIRROR

Hold a mirror close to your mouth and breathe hard on it. Or breathe on a window pane on a cold day. Soon the glass clouds up with tiny drops of water.

3
ICE CUBES
SHINY TIN

Find a clean tin which is shiny on the outside. Fill the tin with ice cubes. After a few minutes, the outside of the tin will be covered with water drops.

Why It Works

When warm air, with lots of water vapour in it, touches something cold, the tiny water drops collect into big drops and you can see them. This is called condensation. When warm air, with lots of water vapour, rises up to meet cold air in the sky, the tiny drops of water collect round specks of dust in the air. As more collect, they make a cloud. If there is enough water in low clouds, it falls as rain.

Dew

The water drops you see on grass and leaves on some mornings are water from the air. During the night the ground gets cold and water vapour collects into drops.

Frost

The white frost you see on a very cold morning on grass or windows is frozen dew. The water which collects on the ground and glass freezes into white ice.

Snow

When air very high in the sky cools quickly, the water in it freezes into crystals and falls as snow. You can see the snow crystals with a magnifying glass.

Water Turbine

Make this Turbine and hold it under a running tap. It will spin round and round as the water spurts out. If you hold the string between your fingers, so it can turn too, the Turbine will spin as long as there is water in it.

You will need
an empty plastic or polythene
    bottle
a pencil
a short bit of string, about 15 cm
    long and a long, thin string,
    about 30 cm long
scissors

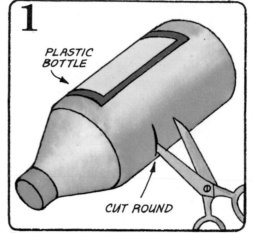

1 PLASTIC BOTTLE — CUT ROUND

Push one blade of the scissors into the bottle, near the top, like this. Snip all the way round to cut the top off.

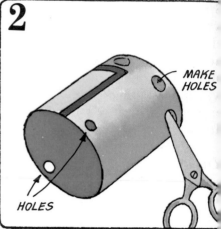

2 MAKE HOLES — HOLES

Make eight holes in the side of th[e] bottle, near the bottom, with scissors. Space them out evenly. Make two holes in the top of the bottle, one on each side.

3 PUSH IN AND PRESS DOWN

Push the point of a pencil into a bottom hole in the bottle. Press the pencil down until it is against the side of the bottle. Do the same with each hole to slant them.

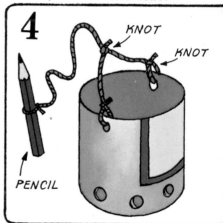

4 KNOT KNOT PENCIL

Tie the ends of the short string to the holes in the top of the bottle. Tie the long string to the middle o[f] the short bit. Tie a pencil to the other end, like this.

Why It Works

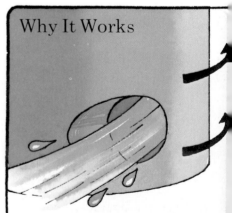

When water squirts out of the holes, it comes out sideways. The jets push the bottle away and make it spin round in the opposite direction.

Turn on the cold tap and hold the bottle, by the string or pencil, under it. As it fills up, the water squirts out the sides and the bottle spins round and round.

HOLD THE TURBINE UNDER A RUNNING TAP TO MAKE IT WORK.

Spin Drier

Spin this little Drier and it will whizz all the water out of wet cloth or wet paper towels. It will not make them completely dry but it will get rid of a lot of water. It is best to do this experiment out of doors where it does not matter if things get wet.

You will need
- a plastic bottle
- a pencil
- a cotton reel
- scissors
- string

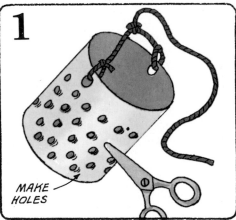

1

MAKE HOLES

Cut off the top of the plastic bottle and tie on strings in the same way as pictures 1 and 2 for the Water Turbine. Poke lots of holes in the bottle with scissors.

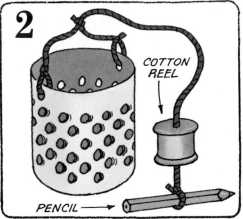

2

COTTON REEL

PENCIL

Slide a cotton reel on to the long string on the bottle. Tie a pencil to the end of the string.

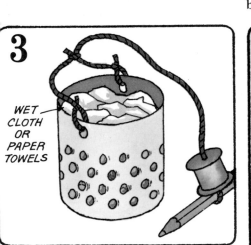

3

WET CLOTH OR PAPER TOWELS

Push bits of wet cloth or wet paper towels into the bottle. Press them down gently. Do not pack them in too tightly.

Did You Know?

Electric spin driers and washing machines work in the same way as your drier. They whizz round very fast and the water in the wet clothes flies out the holes in the drum.

Why It Works

When anything, like this big top, spins things on it are flung off. This is called centrifugal force. When the Drier spins, the water is flung out through the holes.

Hold the cotton reel in one hand. Wind the pencil round and round as fast as you can with the other hand, like this.

If you have one, tie the string to the end of an egg whisk. Wind the handle as fast as you can to spin the Drier. As it spins, water will come out of the holes.

SPIN THE DRIER AS FAST AS YOU CAN.

Science Words

Atmospheric Pressure
This is the pressure of air all round us. At sea level, it is nearly three kilograms per square centimetre but gets less as you go up hills or up in the air. You do not feel this pressure on you because there is equal pressure in your body pushing outwards. The cabins of high-flying aircraft have pressurized air in them. Without this, the passengers would feel very uncomfortable and their noses and ears might bleed.

Carbon Dioxide
This is a gas which is made when you mix together vinegar and baking soda. There are lots of other ways of making it. Carbon dioxide is put into some drinks, such as coco-cola and lemonade, to make them fizzy.

Contraction
This means shrinking or getting smaller. Things such as metal, air and water contract when they are cooled. A steel bridge, $1\frac{1}{2}$ kilometres long, may be as much as a metre shorter on a very cold day than on a hot day.

Condensation
This is the tiny drops of water you see on cold things, such as the bathroom walls when you run the hot tap, or mist on windows on a cold day. Tiny drops of water in warm air, too small to see, condense on something cold and collect into big drops.

Expansion
This means swelling or getting bigger. Lots of things, such as air, metal and water expand when they are warmed. Bridges and railway lines are a bit longer on hot days than on cold ones. Even tall buildings grow a little. The Empire State Building in New York is about 15 cm taller on a hot summer day than on a cold winter day.

Friction
When two things are rubbed together, the rougher they are the more difficult it is for them to slide over each other. This resistance is called friction.

Lubrication
This means putting something, such as oil or grease, on a machine to stop the moving bits rubbing together. The oil keeps the bits slightly apart so they slide easily over each other. If a machine runs without oil, the bits grate together and may get so hot that they melt and stick to each other.

Optical Illusion
This is something you see but which is not really there. Or it may be something which looks different from the way it really is. You see illusions either because your eyes are tricked by them or because what your eyes see is real but the message they give your brain gets muddled up.

Sodium Bicarbonate
This is the chemical name for baking soda. When sodium bicarbonate is stirred into cakes or pastry and then cooked, it gives off carbon dioxide gas. The gas bubbles up through the cake or pastry and makes it light to eat.

Spectrum
This is the name of the seven main colours you see in a rainbow. They are red, orange, yellow, green, blue, indigo and violet. You see these colours when ordinary light, which looks white, is split up into the colours it is made of. When lights of all these colours are shone on the same spot, the spot looks white.

Vibration
This means that something wiggles up and down or backwards and forwards very fast. It may be too fast for you to see it. When anything vibrates you hear a noise, unless the vibration is too small. If you touch anything which is making a noise or music gently with your fingers, you may feel it vibrate.

Water Vapour
When water dries up, it goes into the air in tiny drops, so small you cannot see them. This is called water vapour. Warm, dry air can take up more water than cold damp air. Wet things dry more quickly on warm, dry days than on cold or damp days.

Going Further

If you would like to try more experiments, here are some books about science with experiments in them.

The Young Scientist Book of Jets
by Mark Hewish (Usborne)

The Young Scientist Book of Spaceflight
by Ken Gatland (Usborne)

The Young Scientist Book of Electricity
by Phil Chapman (Usborne)

The Young Scientist Book of the Undersea
by Christopher Pick (Usborne)

The Young Scientist Book of Stars and Planets
by Christopher Maynard (Usborne)

The Book of Experiments
by Leonard de Vries (Carousel Books)

Experiments with Everyday Objects
by Kevin Goldstein-Jackson (Souvenir Press)

Fun with Chemistry
by Mae and Ira Freeman (Kaye and Ward)